John Daudet

A Short and Easy Catechism of the Catholic Religion

John Daudet

A Short and Easy Catechism of the Catholic Religion

ISBN/EAN: 9783337389901

Printed in Europe, USA, Canada, Australia, Japan

Cover: Foto ©Andreas Hilbeck / pixelio.de

More available books at **www.hansebooks.com**

Short and Easy

CATECHISM

—OF THE—

Catholic Religion,

—BY—

. REV. J. D.

PRAYER

Our heavenly Father, we come hither with joy, as to thy school, to hear and learn thy blessed word; we are in thy presence, we know that thou seest us; grant us the grace of assisting with attention, respect and modesty at this Catechism. Adorable Jesus! who didst love children, speak to our hearts in this instruction, for thou hast the words of Eternal life. *Amen.* Our Father, &c. Hail Mary, &c.

AFTER CATECHISM.

Lord Jesus Christ, Son of the living God! we beseech thee through thy holy cross and passion, through thy death and glorious resurrection, be gracious and merciful unto us and all sinners—O Jesus! hear us; O Jesus! save us; O Jesus! have mercy upon us; strengthen our faith; increase our hope, and make us perfect in the love of God and of our neighbor; that in this life we may serve thee alone.

FORMS OF PRAYER THAT ALL CHRISTIANS SHOULD KNOW AND SAY DAILY:

THE SIGN OF THE CROSS.

In the name of the Father, and of the Son, and of the Holy Ghost, *Amen.*

THE LORD'S PRAYER.

Our Father who art in heaven! hallowed be thy name; thy kingdom come; thy will be done on earth, as it is in heaven. Give us this day our daily bread; and forgive us our trespasses, as we forgive them who trespass against us; and lead us not into temptation, but deliver us from evil. *Amen.*

THE ANGELIC SALUTATION.

Hail, Mary, full of grace, the Lord is with thee, blessed art thou among women, and blessed is the fruit of thy womb, Jesus. Holy Mary, Mother of God, pray for us sinners, now, and at the hour of our death. *Amen.*

THE APOSTLES' CREED.

I believe in God, the Father Almighty, Creator of heaven and earth; and in Jesus Christ his only Son, our Lord, who was conceived by the Holy Ghost, born of the Virgin Mary; suffered under Pontius Pilate, was crucified, dead and buried; he descended into hell; the third day he rose again from the dead; he ascended into heaven, sitteth at the right hand of God the Father Almighty; from thence he shall come to judge the living and the dead. I believe in the Holy Ghost; the Holy Catholic Church; the communion of Saints; the Forgiveness of sins, the Resurrection of the body, and Life everlasting. *Amen.*

AN ACT OF FAITH.

O my God! I firmly believe all the sacred truths the Catholic Church believes and teaches, because thou hast revealed them who canst neither deceive nor be deceived.

AN ACT OF HOPE.

O my God! relying upon thy goodness and promises, I hope to obtain grace to serve thee in this world, and life everlasting, through the merits of Jesus Christ, my Lord and Redeemer.

AN ACT OF LOVE.

O my God! I love thee above all things with my whole heart and soul, because thou art infinitely worthy of love; I love also my neighbor as myself, for the love of thee; I forgive all who have injured me, and ask pardon of all whom I have injured.

ACT OF CONTRITION.

O my God! I am most heartily sorry for all my sins, and I detest them, above all things, from the bottom of my heart, because they displease thee, who art most deserving of all my love. I firmly purpose, by thy holy grace, never more to offend thee, and to amend my life.

THE CONFITEOR.

I confess to Almighty God, to the blessed Mary, ever Virgin, to blessed Michael the Archangel, to blessed John the Baptist, to the Holy Apostles, Peter and Paul, and to all the Saints, that I have sinned exceedingly in thought, word and deed, through my fault, through my most grievous fault. Therefore, I beseech the blessed Mary, ever Virgin, blessed Michael the Archangel, blessed John the Baptist, the Holy Apostles, Peter and Paul, and all the Saints, to pray to the Lord our God for me.

May the Almighty God have mercy on me, forgive me my sins, and bring me to everlasting life. *Amen.*

May the Almighty and Merciful Lord give me pardon, absolution, and remission of my sins. *Amen.*

THE ANGELUS.

1. The angel of the Lord declared unto Mary; and she conceived of the Holy Ghost. Hail, Mary, &c.

2. Behold the handmaid of the Lord; be it done unto me according to thy word. Hail, Mary, &c.

3. And the Word was made flesh, and dwelt amongst us. Hail, Mary, &c.

LET US PRAY.

Pour fourth, we beseech thee, O Lord, thy grace into our hearts; that we to whom the Incarnation of Christ, thy Son, was made known by the message of an angel, may by his passion and cross be brought to the glory of his resurrection, through the same Christ our Lord. *Amen*.

BEFORE MEALS, SAY:

Bless us, O Lord! and these thy gifts, which we are about to receive from thy bounty, through Christ our Lord. *Amen*.

AFTER MEALS, SAY:

We give thee thanks, O Almighty God! for all thy benefits, who livest and reignest, world without end. *Amen*.

DECALOGUE.

1. I am the Lord thy God; thou shalt not have strange gods before me.
2. Thou shalt not take the name of God in vain.
3. Thou shalt keep holy the Sabbath day.
4. Honor thy father and mother.
5. Thou shalt not kill.
6. Thou shalt not commit adultery.
7. Thou shalt not steal.
8. Thou shalt not bear false witness against thy neighbor.
9. Thou shalt not covet thy neighbor's wife.
10. Thou shalt not covet thy neighbor's goods.

A Short Form of Confession.

The penitent before entering the confessional examines his conscience on the Commandments of God and of the Church, on the Seven Deadly Sins, &c., excites in his heart sorrow for his sins, and makes a firm resolution to avoid them for the future.

Having knelt down in the Confessional, he makes the sign of the cross and says:

BLESS ME, FATHER, FOR I HAVE SINNED. I CONFESS TO ALMIGHTY GOD AND TO YOU, FATHER.

He then states how long since his last confession, and whether he received absolution and performed his penance. After this he says:

I ACCUSE MYSELF, &C.

Here he mentions his sins, and how often he has committed them since his last confession.

He then says:

FOR THESE SINS AND ALL THE OTHERS I DO NOT NOW REMEMBER, I AM HEARTILY SORRY, AND ASK PARDON OF GOD AND PENANCE AND ABSOLUTION OF YOU, FATHER, IF YOY JUDGE ME WORTHY.

After having humbly listened to the advice of his Confessor, he renews his sorrow and says the Act of Contrition while the Priest gives the absolution.

After retiring from the Confessional, he should spend some time before the altar in making Acts of Thanksgiving.

INTRODUCTION.

Who made you ?
God made me.

What is God ?
God is the Maker and Sovereign Lord of all things.

Why did God make you ?
To know, love and serve him.

What will God give to those who love and serve him ?
Life everlasting.

What is life everlasting ?
A life of a perfect and eternal happiness hereafter.

How do we know how to serve God ?
By the religion.

What is the religion ?
Religion is the whole of the requisites to obtain life everlasting.

How many religions are there ?
There is only one true religion, as there is only one God.

Why do not all men follow the true religion ?
Because, being of free will, some rebel against God and make religions of their own.

Which is the true religion ?
It is that which was revealed by Christ, and handed down to us without change.

How do we call the true religion ?
The Catholic religion.

What does it contain ?
Mysteries, Sacraments and Commandments.

THE FIRST PART.

MYSTERIES.

LESSON I.

What are mysteries?

Mysteries are truths revealed by God, which we believe, though we do not understand.

How can we believe what we do not understand?

We believe, because God is truth itself and cannot deceive us.

How do we know what God has revealed?

By the teaching of the church. (See lessons on the church.)

Is there no particular statement of the mysteries of the religion?

There is one, very ancient, and called the Apostle's Creed.

Say it.

I believe in God &c. (Page 4.)

Which are the chief mysteries of the religion?

The Holy Trinity, the Incarnation and the Redemption.

LESSON II.—THE HOLY TRINITY.

Is there more than one God?

There is only one God, who made heaven and earth and all things.

Had God a beginning?

God had no beginning: he always was and will always be, that is, he is eternal.

Has God a body?
God has not a body: he is pure spirit, and infinitely perfect.

Where is God?
God is everywhere, filling heaven and earth with his presence.

Does God know and see all things?
God knows and sees at once all things past, present and future.

What is the Holy Trinity?
The Holy Trinity is one God in three persons.

Is there three persons in God?
Yes, there are three persons in God: the Father, the Son and the Holy Ghost.

Is the Father God?
The Father is God, the Son is God, the Holy Ghost is God.

Are these Three Divine Persons three Gods?
They are only one God, one Divine Essence.

Which is the most ancient, or the most perfect?
These Three Divine Persons are equal in all.

What is Providence?
Providence is the action of God ruling the world.

LESSON III.—THE CREATION AND MAN.
(Genesis, chapters 1, 2 and 3.)

How long ago was the world created?
About six thousand years ago.

Did God make it all at once?
God could make the world all at once, but he was pleased to make it in six days, and gradually.

Of what did he make it?
Out of nothing, by his word.

What did he create on the first day?
Heaven and earth and the light.

What on the second?
The firmament.

What on the third?
On the third day God separated the waters from the earth, and made the latter produce all kinds of plants and fruits.

What on the fourth?
The sun, the moon and the stars.

What on the fifth?
On the fifth he made the fishes of the sea and the fowls of the air.

What on the sixth?
On the sixth day God made the beasts of the earth, and the last of all, he made man to his image and likeness.

Why did God create man the last?
To show his excellence over the other creatures.

In what is man superior to the other creatures?
In his having a body and an immortal soul, being of free will, capable of knowing God, and destined to life everlasting.

Who was the first man?
Adam.

The first woman?
Eve.

Where did Adam and Eve live in the beginning?
They lived happy in a place of the earth, called the earthly paradise.

Did they preserve their primitive happiness ?
They did not, for they disobeyed God by eating forbidden rruit.

How were they punished?
They were expelled from the earthly paradise, condemned to death, and excluded from heaven.

How is their disobedience called ?
Original sin.

Why ?
Because it passes to their posterity.

Do all men come from Adam and Eve ?
All men come from Adam and Eve.

Are all men born in the state of original sin ?
All men are born in the state of original sin, but Christ and his mother.

LESSON IV.—ANGELS.

(St. Luke, 1 and 2.)

Did God create only man to know, love and serve him ?
God created also angels to know, love and serve him.

What are angels ?
Angels are spirits, not having a body.

How many sorts of angels are there ?
There are two sorts of angels, the good and the bad angels.

Who are the good angels ?
The good angels are those who remained faithful to God when some rebelled.

How were they rewarded for their fidelity ?
They were confirmed forever in grace and glory.

What are they doing ?
They adore God in heaven, and are the ministers of his providence in the world.

Who are the guardian angels ?
The guardian angels are those who take care of man. Every one of us has a guardian angel.

Who are the bad angels ?
They are those who rebelled against God.

How were they punished for their rebellion ?
They were expelled from heaven and condemned to hell.

How are they called ?
Devils.

What are they doing ?
They tempt men on earth by the permission of God, and torment the wicked in hell.

Why do devils tempt us ?
Because they are jealous of our being called to fill their places in heaven.

LESSON V.—THE INCARNATION.

What is the mystery of the Incarnation ?
The mystery of the Incarnation is the Son of God made man.

How was the Son of God made man ?
By taking a soul and a body in the chaste womb of the Blessed Virgin Mary.

How do we call the Son of God made man ?
Jesus Christ.

Is Jesus Christ together God and man ?
Jesus Christ is together God and man, but his divinity
and his humanity are only one person.

How is Christ God ?
Christ is God, because he is truly the second person of
the Holy Trinity.

How is Christ man ?
Christ is man, because he has a body and a soul like
ours.

Has Christ a father ?
Christ has a heavenly father, who is the first person of
the Holy Trinity; but according to flesh, he has no father.
being born of the Blessed Virgin Mary through the opera-
tion of the Holy Ghost.

Where was Christ born ?
In Bethlehem, a small town of Judea.

On what day ?
On Christmas day.

How long did Christ live on earth ?
About thirty-three years.

LESSON VI.

What is the Blessed Virgin ?
The mother of Christ, the very same woman so often
mentioned in the old prophesies.

*Was she born, like the other children of Adam, in the
state of original sin ?*
No, being called to be the mother of Christ, she was
exempt from the stain of original sin.

How do we call that exemption ?
The Immaculate Conception of the Blessed Virgin Mary.

Was the Blessed Virgin Mary exempt only from original sin?

She was also exempt from actual sin, and from all evil inclinations common to humanity.

Was she married?

She was married to St. Joseph, who like her was of the tribe of Judea and of the royal blood of king David.

How can she be called virgin, having been married and being a mother?

She is called virgin, because, though married, she did not cease to live virgin, and, as mother, she conceived of the Holy Ghost and not of man.

Where did she live after her marriage?

She lived thirty years in Nazareth with Jesus and St. Joseph.

Where was she during the public mission of our Divine Savior?

She followed him wherever he went, and was standing by the cross when he died.

What became of her when our Lord had left the earth?

She followed St. John, the apostle, to whose care she had been entrusted by her Divine Son.

Where did she die?

She died in Jerusalem, at the age of seventy-two years, amid the apostles.

Is there any tradition concerning her resurrection?

There always was a tradition prevailing in the church, that she was raised from the dead, three days after her death, and made her ascent into heaven in soul and body.

Why do we call her mother of God?

Because she is truly mother of God, her son, Jesus Christ, being God.

Can you illustrate that by a similitude ?

Yes; the mother of a man who is king is styled mother of the king; so Jesus Christ being God, his mother is mother of God.

LESSON VII.—THE REDEMPTION.

(St. Matt., chs. 26, 27, 28.)

What is the mystery of the Redemption ?

The mystery of the Redemption is the restoration of man to his primitive destiny by the sufferings and death of Christ.

What was the primitive destiny of man ?

The primitive destiny of man was, after having lived some time on earth, to go to heaven and possess life everlasting.

How did man lose his primitive destiny ?

By original sin.

Could not man before Christ go to heaven ?

No man before Christ could go to heaven.

And now can we go to heaven ?

All men now can go to heaven, having been redeemed by Christ.

How did Christ suffer, as man or as God ?

Christ suffered only as man, because God cannot suffer nor die.

But if Christ suffered only as man, how could he redeem mankind ?

Christ, as God, gave an infinite merit to his sufferings, and thereby full satisfaction to the divine justice for all men.

What kind of death did he suffer ?

He was crucified.

On what day did Christ die ?
On Good Friday.

What became of his body ?
His body was taken down fiom the cross and buried by his Apostles and disciples.

What became of his soul ?
His soul descended into limbo to deliver the saints of the ancient law.

What was limbo ?
A place where the souls of the just before Christ were detained until the Redemption.

———

LESSON VIII.—THE RESURRECTION AND THE ASCENSION.

What did happen on the third day after Christ's death?
He rose from the dead, uniting again his body to his soul.

On what day ?
On Easter Sunday.

How long did Christ remain on earth after his resurrection ?
He remained 40 days, during which he often appeared to his Disciples, and gave his last instructions to his Apostles.

When did he leave the earth ?
On the Ascension day.

Where did he go ?
He ascended into heaven, where he is sitting at the right hand of God.

Has God any right hand?
God has no right nor left hand, but we mean that Chris', as God, is equal to his heavenly Father, and, as mar, he shares in the glory of the Divinity.

Where is Christ now?
Christ, as God, is everywhere; as man, he is in heaven and in the Holy Eucharist.

Will Christ no more appear visibly on earth?
He will come at the end of the world with great majesty, to judge the living and the dead.

On what day did he send the Holy Ghost to his Apostles?
On Pentecost day.

And to what purpose?
To confirm them in their mission and give them a new mark of the divine assistance.

LESSON IX.—THE CHURCH.

How do we know with certainty what God revealed?
By the Church.

How do we receive the benefit of the Redemption?
By the church.

What is the Church?
The church is a society, established by Christ, of all those who believe and profess his doctrine.

How did Christ establish the church?
By appointing a permanent body of pastors, whom He commanded all men to hear and obey.

What conditions are requisite to be a member of the church?
Three conditions are requisite : faith, baptism and submission to the lawful pastors.

Who were the first pastors of the church?
The Apostles.

On what particular occasion were they made pastors?
When Christ said to them : "All power is given to me
'in heaven and in earth. Going therefore, teach all na-
'tions ; baptizing them in the name of the Father, and of
'the Son, and of the Holy.Ghost, teaching them to ob-
'serve all things whatsoever I have commanded to you ;
'and behold I am with you all days, even to the consum-
'mation of the world."—(Matt. xxvii : 18, 19, 20.)

LESSON X.—THE CHURCH CONTINUED.

Who are now the pastors of the church?
The Pope and the Bishops, as the right successors of
the Apostles.

What does Pope mean?
Universal pastor.

Who was the first Pope?
St. Peter.

When was he appointed Pope?
When he received from Christ, with the keys of the
kingdom of heaven, a general jurisdiction.—(St. Matt.
xvi : 18, 19.)

Why is the Bishop of Rome the Pope?
Because St. Peter had his see in Rome, and died Bishop of Rome.

What means Bishop?
Regular pastor.

Who were the first Bishops?
The Apostles.

What are Priests?
Priests are the deputies of the Bishops, from whom they
derive their jurisdiction.

What is the duty of the Pastors?
The duty of the pastors is threefold: 1st, to teach the religion; 2d, to administer the sacraments; 3d, to guide the faithful in the way of salvation.

What is the duty of the faithful?
The duty of the faithful is likewise threefold: 1st, to hear their pastors; 2d, to receive the sacraments at their hands; 3d, to obey them in religious matters.

Is the church infallible?
Yes, the church is and must be infallible in matter of faith, because Christ commanded all men to receive her teaching under penalty of damnation.—(St. Mark xvi, 15.)

How is the church infallible?
The church is infallible, 1st, in the general teaching of ner pastors; 2d, in the decisions of the general or ecumenical councils; 3d, in the solemn decisions of the Pope.

What is a council?
An assembly of bishops convened for regulating religious matters.

When is a council general or ecumenical?
When all the bishops are convened and presided over by the Pope.

———

LESSON XI.—THE MARKS OF THE TRUE CHURCH.

Is there any mark or character of the true chruch?
There are four marks or characters of the true church.

Which are they?
One, Holy, Catholic and Apostolic.

What does One mean?
One means that the true church must be one body, with one head, having everywhere same constitution, same faith, same sacraments.

What does Holy mean?
Holy means that the true church must promote virtue and holiness in an eminent degree.

What does Catholic mean?
Catholic means that the true church must teach all men, maintain the whole doctrine of Christ and never fail in the course of time.

What does Apostolic mean?
Apostolic means that the true church, in her doctrine and hierarchy, must descend from the Apostles, without change or interruption.

Can the Catholic church claim all these marks?
Yes, she can claim all these marks, for
1st, She is one body, with one head, and she has everywhere same constitution, same faith, same sacraments.

2d, No where else is to be found so much good, chastity, charity and devotedness.

3d, She teaches all men, being spread all over the world, maintains the whole doctrine of Christ, and did never fail.

4th, She traces her teaching and hierarchy to the Apostles, without change or interruption.

———

LESSON XII.—THE HOLY SCRIPTURES.
What is the Bible?
The Bible is a book containing the writings of inspired and holy men.

How is the Bible divided ?
The Bible is divided into two parts : The Old and the New Testament.

What does the Old Testament contain ?
The Old Testament contains the Holy Scriptures before Christ.

What does the New Testament contain ?
The New Testament contains the Holy Scriptures after Christ.

Are the Holy Scriptures the word of God ?
Yes, the Holy Scriptures are the word of God, but the meaning is given by the church, as there are things in them hard to be understood.—[II Peter 3.]

How do we know that the Holy Scriptures are inspired, and the word of God ?
We know it only by the church.

What does St. Paul say of the Holy Scriptures ?
He says that they are profitable to teach, and thereby makes us understand that they are particularly intended for the pastors.—[II Tim. 3, 16.]

Is it necessary to read the Holy Scriptures ?
There is no commandment to read them, neither from God nor from the church.

Are the faithful allowed to read the Holy Scriptures ?
Not only the faithful are allowed, but also they are invited to read the Holy Scriptures, provided they do it with a spirit of humility and submission to the decisions of the church.

———

LESSON XIII.—GRACE AND COMMUNION OF SAINTS.

Which is the fruit of the Redemption ?
The fruit of the Redemption is grace.

What is grace ?

Grace is a divine gift, granted through the merits of Christ, for salvation purposes.

How many sorts of grace are there ?

There are two sorts of grace, actual and sanctifying grace.

What is actual grace ?

Actual grace is a divine assistance to do good and keep from sin.

Is actual grace necessary ?

Without grace we cannot keep from sin, nor perform good works, nor acquire any Christian virtue.

What is the Catholic doctrine concerning faith, hope and charity ?

These virtues are divine gifts, poured fourth in our hearts by the Holy Ghost.—Rom. v : 5.]

Does God always grant us sufficient grace to obey his commandments, or resist temptation ?

Yes, God always grants us sufficient grace, but we can obtain more by prayer and good disposition.

What is sanctifying grace ?

Sanctifying grace is our spiritual union to Christ.

When are we in the state of sanctifying grace ?

We are in the state of sanctifying grace when we are free from mortal sin.

What is the effect of sanctifying grace ?

It makes us pleasing to God, and our good works meritorious,

What does it follow from our union to Christ by sanctifying grace ?

It follows that we are united also to the saints in heaven and to the souls in purgatory, forming together a spiritual body, called the Communion of Saints.

How is sanctifying grace acquired?
By baptism.

How is sanctifying grace recovered when lost?
By Penance.

———

LESSON XIV.—THE FOUR LAST THINGS.

What is death?
Death is the separation of our soul from our body.

Is it all at an end with us when we die?
No, there is another life, because our soul is immortal.

What becomes of our body after death?
It is decomposed and turned into dust.

What becomes of our soul?
It appears before God for judgment.

What is that judgment?
A sentence of God fixing our condition for all eternity.

Is there not to be another judgment?
Yes, there will be another, at the end of the world, called the general judgment, confirming the former.

Where do we go after the judgment?
To heaven, to hell or to purgatory.

What is heaven?
A place of bliss, where the just see God and are quite happy for all eternity.

Who are those who go to heaven?
Those who die free from all sin and debt to the divine justice.

What is hell?
A place of woe and torment, where the wicked are punished during all eternity.

Who are the wicked who go to hell?
Those who die in the state of mortal sin.

What is purgatory?
A place where souls are detained and suffer till they obtain admittance into heaven.

Who are those who go to purgatory?
Those who die in venia'. sin, or with any debt to the divine justice.

Can we relieve the souls in purgatory?
Yes, we can relieve them, by prayer, good works, and particularly by the Holy Sacrifice of the Mass.

LESSON XV.—THE END OF THE WORLD.

Will the world last forever?
It will come to an end, preceded by frightful signs.

What will then take place?
The resurrection of the body and the general judgment.

What is the resurrection of the body?
It is the coming again of all men to life with their souls and bodies.

Why will there be a general judgment?
To avenge the justice of God, and confound iniquity.

How will that judgment be carried on?
Jesus Christ will come down from heaven with great majesty, and all men, who ever lived, will appear before him, the just on his right hand, and the wicked on his left hand.

What will the Sovereign Judge say to the just?
Come, ye blessed of my Father, possess you the kingdom prepared for you from the foundation of the world.

What will he say to the wicked?
Depart from me, you cursed, into everlasting fire,
which was prepared for the devil and his angels.—[St.
Matt. ch. xxv.]

SECOND PART.

SACRAMENTS.

LESSON I.

*How does the church give us the benefit of the Redemp-
tion?*
By the sacraments.

What is a sacrament?
A sacrament is a sacred rite, instituted by Christ to
convey grace to our soul.

How many sacraments are there?
There are seven sacraments: Baptism, Confirmation,
Holy Eucharist, Penance, Extreme-Onetion, Holy Order
and Matrimony.

*Do the sacraments convey grace whenever we receive
them?*
They convey grace only when they are received in due
disposition.

Are all the sacraments to be received several times ?
Some are to be received only once; some very often; some in particular circumstances of life.

Which are received only once ?
Baptism, Confirmation and Holy Order.

Why ?
Because they imprint on the soul a character which is for all eternity.

Which are designed specially for forgiving sins ?
Baptism and Penance.

How are they called ?
The sacraments of the dead ; because they rescue us from the death of sin.

How do you call the others ?
The sacraments of the living ; because they are only for those who possess the life of grace.'

What sacrament is to be received the first ?
Baptism, which is as it were the door of the church.

LESSON II.—BAPTISM.

What is Baptism ?
Baptism is a sacrament by which we are released from original sin, made children of God and members of the church.

Does Baptism remit only original sin ?
It remits all sins.

Does anything of sin remain after baptism ?
After baptism nothing remains of sin, neither guilt nor penalty.

Is baptism very necessary ?

Baptism is so very necessary that even infants who die unbaptised cannot enter into heaven.

What did our Savior say to urge the necessity of baptism ?

Unless a man be born again of water and the Holy Ghost, he cannot enter into the kingdom of God. (St. John III: 5.)

Who are the right ministers of baptism ?

The right ministers of baptism are the priests, but in the case of necessity anybody can baptise.

How is baptism given ?

Baptism is given by pouring true water on the receiver, and saying at the same time : I baptise thee in the name of the Father, and of the Son, and of the Holy Ghost.

On which part of the body is the water to be poured ?

On the head as much as possible.

Are the ceremonies of the ritual necessary ?

They are not necessary for the validity of the sacrament, but they are ordered by the church, and it is a sin to neglect them.

What is to be done when an infant receives private baptism ?

The infant must be brought to church, and the ceremonies be supplied as soon as possible.

Is it a sin for parents to delay the christening of their children ?

Yes, it is a great sin, because they expose them to be deprived of seeing God.

Where do infants go when they die unbaptised ?

They go neither to heaven nor to hell, but to a place where they are deprived of seeing God.

LESSON III.—CONFIRMATION.

What is confirmation ?
Confirmation is a sacrament by which we receive the Holy Ghost and are fortified in faith.

Was that sacrament in use in the beginning of the church ?
We see by the Acts that the Apostles were administering it to the faithful.

Is confirmation very necessary for salvation ?
Confirmation is not necessary for salvation, as Baptism is, but it is tempting God to neglect when we have an opportunity to receive it.

What dispositions are requisite to receive it ?
The dispositions requisite are to be in the state of grace, well instructed in the religion, and ready to follow the inspirations of the Hoty Ghost.

Who are the right ministers of confirmation ?
The Bishops.

How does a bishop give confirmation ?
By imposing his hands, invoking the Holy Ghost and annointing our forehead with Holy Chrism.

What is Holy Chrism ?
It is a mixture of balsam and olive oil, blessed by the Bishop on Good Thursday.

What does it signify ?
It signifies the good odor of the christian virtues we are to practice, and the grace of fortitude we receive by the sacrament.

Why does the bishop give a little blow on the cheek ?
To remind us that, being made soldiers of Christ, we must be ready to suffer persecuticn and derision for his sake.

LESSON IV.—HOLY EUCHARIST.

What is the Holy Eucharist?
The Holy Eucharist is a sacrament that contains the true body and the true blood of Jesus Christ, under the appearance of bread and wine.

Does the Holy Eucharist contain only the body and blood af Jesus Christ.
It contains also his soul and his divinity, which cannot be separated from his body and blood.

What effect does that sacrament produce?
It maintains and perfects our spiritual union to Christ.

When did Christ institute the Holy Eucharist?
Christ instituted the Holy Eucharist at his Last Supper, when he changed bread and wine into his body and blood, and said to his apostles : Do this in commemoration of me.   (St. Luke XXII.)

Who can make the Holy Eucharist?
Only those who are duly ordained priests, can make the Holy Eucharist.

Where is that sacrament made?
It is made at the mass.

What is requisite to make it?
Bread and wine.

What becomes of the bread and wine at the mass!
The bread and wine at the mass are really and substantially changed into the body and blood of Jesus Christ.

At what moment of the mass?
At the moment of the consecration, when the priest says in the name of Jesus Christ, THIS IS MY BODY, THIS IS MY BLOOD.

How do we call that wonderful change?
TRANSUBSTANTIATION.

What remains of the bread and wine after the consecration?
After the consecration, nothing remains of the bread and wine but the appearances.

What are appearances?
Appearances are shape, color and taste.

How long does Jesus Christ remain in the Holy Eucharist?
Jesus Christ remains really present in the Holy Eucharist as long as the appearances continue to subsist.

Is not Jesus Christ divided in the Holy Eucharist, his body being on one side and his blood on the other?
Jesus Christ is not divided in the Holy Eucharist, but he is really and wholly present in each kind.

When the priest divides the consecrated host, or the precious blood, does he not divide Jesus Christ?
The priest does not divide Jesus Christ, who remains entire and whole in every part of each kind.

LESSON V.—MASS.

Is the Holy Eucharist only a sacrament?
It is also a sacrifice, which we call MASS.

What is a sacrifice?
A solemn offering to God, in acknowledgement of his supreme and absolute dominion.

What is required for a sacrifice?
A victim whose life is offered to God.

Was Christ's death a sacrifice?
It is the only true sacrifice that was ever offered to God.

Why?
Because all the other sacrifices, practiced of old, were mere figures of that of the cross.

What did Christ offer to God on the cross?
He offered to God his life and sufferings for our redemption, being at once sacrificer and victim.

How is the mass a sacrsfice?
The mass is a sacrifice because it is the continuation of the sacrifice of the cross.

What does Christ offer to God at the mass?
He offers his same body that was crucified, and his same blood that was shed.

Who is the sacrificer at the mass, Christ or the Priest?
Christ is the sacrificer, and the priest only his minister.

What is the merit of a mass?
The merit of a single mass is infinite as well as that of the cross.

How should we attend to the mass?
We should attend with the same respect and the same awe as if we were standing by the cross and looking at Jesus crucified.

LESSON VI.—COMMUNION.

What is communion?
Communion is the receiving of the sacrament of the Holy Eucharist.

How many sorts of communion are there?
There are three sorts of communion: worthy, luke warm, and sacrilegious comununion.

When is communion worthy ?
When it is made in the state of grace, and with due
preparation and devotion.

When is communion lukewarm ?
When it is made without sufficient preparation nor devotion.

When is communion sacrilegious ?
When it is made in the state of mortal sin.

*What does St. Paul say of those who make sacrilegious
communions ?*
He says that they are guilty of the body and blood of
the Lord, and eat and drink judgment to themselves. (I
Corinth., XI.)

*Are there any dispositions of the body requisite for
communion ?*
Yes, there are two dispositions of the body requisite for
communion: full fasting from previous midnight, and
pious manners.

When should we communicate ?
We should very often communicate according to the
ordinance of Christ, who made us understand that communion is for our soul what nourishment is for our body.

Which is the ordinance of the church ?
The ordinance of the church is that we communicate
on Easter time, and whenever we are dangerously sick.

How is the communion of the sick called ?
VIATICUM, which means provision for the journey to
eternity.

Are the sick obliged to be fasting ?
The sick are exempt from fasting when they take the
viaticum.

LESSON VII.—PENANCE.

What is penance ?
Penance is a sacrament that remits our sins after baptism.

When did Christ institute that sacrament ?
Christ instituted that sacrament when he gave power to his apostles to forgive or retain sins. (John XX.)

When do we receive it ?
We receive it when a priest, duly approved, gives us absolution.

What is absolution ?
Absolution is a sentence by which a priest, in the name of Christ, remits our sins.

Does absolution, like baptism, remove everything of sin ?
Absolution removes the guilt as well as the eternal penalty of sin, but it leaves a temporal punishment for this or the other life.

What is requisite to receive penance ?
Three things are requisite: confession, contrition, and satisfaction, which are called the essential parts of the sacrament.

———

What is confession ?
Confession is a declaration of all our sins to a priest, in order to obtain absolution.

What must confession be to be good ?
Confession, to be good, must be humble, sincere, and entire.

What must we do before confession ?
We must examine seriously our conscience.

Is confession good when grievous sins are forgotten?
Confession cannot be good if grievous sins are omitted for want of examination or recollection.

When there is no fault of ours, are forgotten sins forgiven?
Forgotten sins, then, are forgiven as well as the others; however, they must be brought in a next confession.

What is contrition?
Contrition is a hearty sorrow for having offended God, with a firm purpose not to offend him again.

What must contrition be to be good?
It must be interior, supernatural, universal and sovereign.

When is contrition interior?
When it does exist truly in our heart.

When is it supernatural?
When it proceeds from religious motives.

Which are the most usual motives of contrition?
The deformity of sin, the fear of damnation, the goodness of God, and the passion of Christ.

When is contrition universal?
When it reaches all our grievous sins.

When is it sovereign?
When it is stronger than all natural feelings and worldly attractions.

What is satisfaction?
Satisfaction is the reparation we owe to God and to the neighbor for our sins.

How do we give satisfaction to God ?
By humbly accepting the temporal punishment that remains after absolution, and taking efficacious measures to prevent relapsing into sin.

How do we give satisfaction to our neighbor ?
By repairing, as far as possible, the injury or damage, spiritual and temporal, caused by our sins.

What is the penance that we receive in confession ?
It is a good work enjoined by our confessor, for the satisfaction we owe to God.

Which is the benefit of that penance ?
It is easier and more meritorious than anything else we can do.

Are we obliged to fulfill it ?
Yes, we are obliged to fulfill it, because it is a part of the sacrament.

How do pious people fulfill their penance ?
Pious people never remit their penance from day to day, but fulfill it without delay, in order to secure all the fruit of the sacrament.

Is there no possibility to be reconciled to God without confession nor absolution, when there is no priest at hand ?
In case of necessity, we can be reconciled to God by a perfect contrition, including the desire of the sacrament.

When is contrition perfect ?
Contrition is perfect when it is very strong, and proceeds merely from the love of God.

If we can be reconciled to God by a perfect contrition, where is the benefit of the sacrament ?
In the sacrament, so perfect a contrition is not required.

LESSON VIII.—INDULGENCES.

What are indulgences?
Indulgences are the remission of the temporal punishment due to sin.

By whom are indulgences granted?
Indulgences are granted by the pastors of the church, but particularly by the pope.

When did Christ give such a power to his church?
Christ gave that power to his church when he said to his apostles: Whatsoever you shall loose upon earth shall be loosed also in heaven.—(St. Math. XVIII, 18.)

How many sorts of indulgences are there?
There are two sorts of indulgences: plenary and partial indulgences.

What are plenary indulgences?
Plenary indulgences are those that are granted with the intent to remit all temporal penalty of sin.

What are partial indulgences?
Partial indulgences are those that are limited in their extent, according to certain rules received in the church.

What is a jubilee?
A jubilee is a plenary indulgence, granted with more solemnity than usually.

What is requisite to gain indulgences!
Two conditions are requisite: First, to be in the state of grace; Second, to fulfill everything that is prescribed.

May we apply the indulgences to the souls in purgatory?
Yes, we may, particularly those that are designed for it, but only by mere suffrage.

What do you mean by mere suffrage?
We mean that God, then, is not bound to grant our request, though it is very agreeable to him.

LESSON IX.—EXTREME UNCTION.

What is extreme unction?

It is a sacrament that gives us comfort and relief in sickness, both for the soul and body.

What does St. James say of this sacrament, in his epistle?

He says: is any man sick among you, let him bring in the priests of the church, and let them pray over him, annointing him with oil in the name of the Lord, and the prayer of the faith shall save the sick man, and the Lord shall raise him up; and if he be in sins they shall be forgiven him.—(James v.)

What relief does that sacrament give to the soul?

It increases sanctifying grace, and gives us the special graces we want in sickness, of patience, resignation, and strength to overcome temptations.

What relief does it give to the body?

It often soothes our pains, and sometimes restores us to health, if expedient for our spiritual welfare.

How does it forgive sins?

It forgives sins by supplying to some extent, and in some cases, the sacrament of penance.

When should we receive that sacrament?

When we are in danger of death by sickness.

How to receive it with a better fruit?

We must send for the priest in time, and not wait till we are deprived of our senses.

———

LESSON X.—HOLY ORDER.

What is Holy Order?

Holy order is a sacrament that confers the character of priesthood, and gives grace to discharge the functions of the ministry.

When did Christ institute holy order?
Christ instituted holy order at His Last Supper, when He command His Apostles to offer the holy sacrifice of the mass.

How many degrees of priesthood are there?
There are two degrees of priesthood: bishops and priests.

How do they differ?
They differ in two points.

Which is the first?
Bishops are the regular pastors and rulers of the church; priests are only deputies, and cannot exercise the ministry but under the rule of the bishops.

Which is the second?
Bishops have power to administer all the sacraments; priests cannot give confirmation nor holy order.

Is it a great sin to fail in respect to a priest?
Yes, it is a great sin, because priests are the anointed of the Lord, and the representatives of Christ.

What does St. Bernard say of priests?
He says: God preferred them to angels.

———

LESSON XI.—MATRIMONY.

What is matrimony?
Matrimony, as a Sacrament, is the christian marriage.

What is marriage?
Marriage is the union of a man and a woman as heads of family.

Who instituted marriage?
God Himself instituted marriage, when, in the beginning of the world, He commanded man and woman to live together in family.

What did Christ for marriage?
Christ raised the marriage of Christians to the dignity of a sacrament.

What effects does the sacrament produce?
It makes the union of spouses holy, and gives them daily graces to discharge their duties as heads of family.

In what dispositions should those who contract marriage be?
They should be in the state of grace, and well instructed in religion.

How should married people live to obtain the daily graces of matrimony.
They should live in modesty, charity, piety, and be very zealous for the education of their children.

How is marriage contracted?
Marriage is contracted by a free, lawful and mutual consent.

When is marriage consent lawful?
When it is in accordance with the regulations of the church.

What are those regulations?
They are of two kinds: prohibitions and impediments.

What do prohibitions purport?
They forbid marrying in certain cases or without certain conditions, but if not complied with, they do not make the marriage void, only sinful.

What do impediments purport?
Impediments make marriage void.

Does not the church sometimes dispense with those pro-hibitions or impediments?

Yes, she sometimes dispenses, but she always requires good and strong reasons.

Can marriage be dissolved?

Marriage can never be dissollved, for Christ said: What God has joined together, let no man put asunder. (Mat. xix: 6.)

THIRD PART.

--

COMMANDMENTS.

LESSON I.

Is it enough for salvation to believe the mysteries of the religion?

We must also obey its commandments, because faith without works is dead.—(St. James ii. 26.)

What are commandments?

Commandments are rules of conduct, either from God or from the church.

How many commandments of God are there?

There are ten commandments of God, called DECA-LOGUE. (See p. 6.)

When did God reveal those commandments?

God revealed them first to Adam, then to Moses, and finally they were explained and confirmed by Jesus Christ.

How many commandments of the church are there?

They are many, but those concerning the community at large may be reduced to six.

Do the commandments of the church oblige us as well as those of God?

The commandments of the church oblige us as well as those of God; for Christ said to his apostles: "He that heareth you, heareth me; he that despiseth you, despiseth me." (St. Luke, x. 16.)

LESSON II.—DECALOGUE.

Which is the first commandment of God?

I am the Lord thy God; thou shalt have no strange gods before me.

What does that commandment prescribe?

It prescribes to adore God alone, as the sovereign Lord of all things and the source of all good.

How do we adore God?

By faith, hope and charity.

What is faith?

Faith is a firm ascent to whatever God revealed, relying on his veracity and the teaching of the church. (See lesson on grace.)

What is hope?

Hope is an entire reliance on the bounty of God and the merits of Christ for salvation and the means of salvation.

What is charity?

Charity is loving God above all and our neighbor as ourselves for God's sake.

When do we truly love God?

When we seek to please him in all our actions, and are ready to part with everything or every one, rather than to offend him.

Who is the neighbor?
The neighbor is all mankind, that is to say, we must love all men without exception.

Must we love all men equally?
We may, and must love more some than others, according to relationship or friendship.

Must we love our enemies?
We must love our enemies, do good to them, and never revenge.

What did our Savior say on that subject?
" Love your enemies, do good to them that hate you, and pray for them that persecute you. (St. Matt. VII. 12.)

When do we truly love the neighbor?
When we do to the others whatsoever we would they should do to us in like circumstances.

LESSON III.

By what practical means are we to adore God?
By prayer and deeds of charity.

What do you understand by deeds of charity?
Anything by which we relieve the temporal and spiritual wants of the neighbor.

What is prayer?
An humble petition to God.

Is prayer only a petition?
It is also any act of faith, hope and charity.

How must prayer he done to be acceptable to God?
It must be done with attention, devotion, perseverance and humility.

How often should we pray?
Our Savior said that we should pray at all times. (St.
Luke XXI. 36.)

How can we pray at all times?
By offering to God all our actions.

How is praying performed?
By way of meditation, or by using the forms of prayer
approved by the church.

Did not our Savior himself give a form of prayer?
He gave one, called the Lord's prayer, which all Chris-
tions should know.

Say it.
Our Father, &c. (See p. 4.)

Is it sufficient to adore God individually and privately?
We owe to God also a public and solemn worship, to
which every one must attend and contribute.

Where does that public worship take place?
In churches.

*What are good Christians wont to do in reference to
the first commandment?*
They say prayers night and morning, offer their actions
to God from time to time during the day, attend regularly
to the offices of the church, and contribute to the expenses
of the religion according to their means and the rules of
each diocese.

How do we break that commandment?
By idolatry, superstition, fortune-telling, magical prac-
tices, and finally, by neglecting prayer and church.

———

LESSON IV.—DECALOGUE.

What is idolatry?
Idolatry is worshipping creatures as gods, or like God.

May we, however, worship angels and saints?
We ought to worship angels and saints, but not like God.

What kind of worship do we owe them?
A worship relating to God.

May we pray them?
Yes, we may pray them to join and support our prayers before God.

Is it not injurious to the mediation of Christ?
No more than to claim the prayers of our brethren, as very often does St. Paul in his epistles.

What saint is the most deserving our worship and confidence.
The Blessed Virgin Mary.

Do we not go too far in our devotion to the Blessed Virgin?
We only obey the commandment of the Holy Ghost, who made her say: All generations shall call me blessed. (St. Luke, i. 48.)

What do you say of relics and images?
We ought to venerate relics and holy images for what they represent, and the holy thoughts they convey to mind.

Is it not forbidden by the first commandment of God to make use of images or graven things?
It is forbiden to adore images, as do idolaters, but it is not forbidden to make use of them.

Can you prove it?
There were, by a special order of God, images on the arc of the testimony, (Exod. xxv. 22,) and in the temple of Solomon. (iii Kings, vi. 27.)

LESSON V.—DECALOGUE—2D AND 3D COMMANDMENTS OF GOD.

Which is the second commandment of God?
Thou shalt not take the name of God in vain.

What does that commandment forbid?
It forbids us using the name of God, or any sacred name, disrespectfully.

How do we break that commandment?
By cursing, blaspheming, swearing. violating our vows, and by perjury.

What is swearing?
Swearing, or making an oath, is an appeal to God for the truth of what we say.

Is all swearing bad?
All swearing is not bad, but private and indiscreet swearing.

When is swearing licit?
When it is for a grave cause, or at the request of a superior.

When sworn, are we obliged to say truth?
Yes, we are obliged to say truth, and the whole truth, cost what it may.

What is perjury?
Perjury is a false oath.

Is perjury a crime?
Perjury is one of the greatest crimes that man can commit.

Which is the third commandment of God?
Tho sha't keep holy the sabbath day.

What does that commandment prescribe?
To appropriate all Sundays for the public service of God.

What must we do on Sunday ?
We must rest from manual work, if not necessary, keep from profane amusements, and attend to church.

———

LESSON VI. — DECALOGUE — 4TH, 5TH AND 6TH COMMANDMENTS OF GOD.

Which is the fourth commandment of God ?
Honor thy father and mother, that thou mayest live a long time.

What does that commandment prescribe ?
To love, obey, respect, and if necessary, support your parents.

What else does that commandment prescribe ?
It prescribes also to respect and obey our temporal and spiritual superiors.

———

Which is the fifth commandment of God ?
Thou shalt not kill.

What does that commandment forbid ?
Murder, suicide, and doing any injury to human body, as well as fighting, quarreling, hatred and revenge.

Does that commandment forbid only the murder of the body ?
It forbids, also, the murder of the soul, that is to say, scandal.

What is scandal ?
Scandal is anything by which we induce others to sin.

———

Which is the sixth commandment of God ?
Thou shalt not commit adultery.

What does that commandment forbid?
It forbids lust and every thing conducive to it, like in-temperance, idleness, bad company, improper familiarities, immodest conversations, and so forth.

What virtue is opposite to lust ?
Chastity.

Which are the ordinary means to preserve or acquire chastity ?
Prayer, modesty, mortification, frequent confession and communion.

———

LESSON VII.—DECALOGUE—7TH, 8TH, 9TH AND 10TH COMMANDMENTS OF GOD.

Which is the seventh commandment of God?
Thou shalt not steal.

What does that commandment forbid?
It forbids all unjust taking away or keeping what belongs to others, as well as wronging anybody.

What must we do when we have committed any theft, robbery, cheating or swindling ?
We must make restitution, because thieves cannot go to heaven.

What must we do when we have wronged somebody ?
We must pay or repair the damage as for as possible.

When we find money, or any thing valuable, can we appropriate it to ourselves?
It must be restored to the owner, and if the owner is not known, we are bound to make sufficient inquiries.

———

Which is the eighth commandment of God?
Thou shalt not bear false witness against thy neighbor.

What does that commandment forbid?
It forbids telling lies, detraction, calumny, and rash judgment.

Can a lie be a mortal sin?
Yes, when it deceives or injures the neighbor in a serious manner.

———

Which is the ninth commandment of God?
Thou shalt not covet thy neighbor's wife.

What does that commandment forbid?
It forbids willful desires of lust.

Does it not forbid also impure thoughts?
It forbids also impure thoughts, because they engender bad desires.

Is a lewd desire less sinful than a bad action?
There is no difference before God.

———

Which is the tenth commandment of God?
Thou shalt not covet thy neighbor's goods.

What does that commandment forbid?
It forbids envy, jealousy, covetousness, and all desire to acquire riches by unlawful means.

— — —

LESSON VIII.—COMMANDMENTS OF THE CHURCH.

Which are the most usual commandments of the church?
1. To hear mass on Sundays and holy-days.
2. To keep holy, like Sundays, the feasts of obligation.
3. To confess at least once a year.
4. To make the holy communion at Easter.
5. To fast on Lent, Ember days, Vigils, and Fridays of advent.
6. To abstain from flesh meat all Fridays and also on fasting days when there is no dispensation of the bishop.

Which are the feasts of obligation that fall on week days?
1. The circumcision; 2, the epiphany; 3, the annunciation; 4, the ascension; 5, corpus christi; 6, the assumption; 7, all saints; 8, the immaculate conception; 9, Christmas.

At what age do we begin to be bound to fast?
At the age of 21 years.

What are the ordinary reasons which dispense from fasting?
Sickness, old age, hard labor, nursing and pregnancy.

LESSON IX.—SIN.

What is it when we break a commandment?
It is sin.

What does sin mean?
Disobedience or rebellion to God.

Are all sin equal?
Some are mortal, some venial.

What is a mortal sin?
A wilful and grievous transgression of the law of God.

What injury does it cause?
It deprives us altogether of sanctifying grace.

Why is it called mortal or deadly sin?
Because it is·a spiritual death, breaking our union to Christ.

What punishment does it deserve?
The eternal pains of hell.

What is a venial sin?
It is likewise a transgression of the law of God, but not grievous or quite wilful.

What injury does it cause?
It diminishes sanctifying grace and disposes us to mortal sin.

What punishment does it deserve?
A temporal punishment, which is to be suffered in this life by a voluntary penance, or hereafter in purgatory.

What are capital sins?
They are evil inclinations, to which, as to their source, all sins are referred, according to their predominant malice.

How many are they?
Seven : pride, covetousness, lust, envy, gluttony, anger and sloth.

LESSON X.—GOOD WORKS.

What are good works?
Good works are actions performed in accordance with the law of God or with the evangelical counsels.

What benefit is there in doing good works?
We secure a reward in heaven for every good work we do.

Is there nothing requisite to make our good works meritorious?
We must be in the state of grace and have a pure intention.

Are the good works of sinners destitute of all merit?
They are not meritorious for heaven, but they serve to propitiate the mercy of God.

What are virtues?
Habits of doing good.

How do we acquire the christian virtues?
By practice, but particularly by the grace of God. Some are mere gifts of God.

How many sorts of virtues are there?
There are two sorts of virtues: The theological and the moral virtues.

Which are the former ?
Faith, hope and charity.   (See page 4.)

Why are they called theological ?
Because their immediate object is God himself.

Are they most necessary for salvation ?
There is nothing more necessary.

LESSON XI.

What are the moral virtues ?
Good habits relating to morals.

How are they divided ?
Into three classes : 1st, the cardinal virtues ; 2d, the capital virtues ; 3d, the virtues of perfection.

Which are the cardinal virtues?
Prudence, justice, temperance and fortitude.

What is prudence ?
The habit of being considerate in all things.

What is justice ?
The habit of giving each one his due.

What is temperance or moderation ?
The habit of keeping from extremes and excesses.

What is fortitude ?
The habit of being steadfast and persevering in our resolutions and enterprises.

Why are they called cardinal?
Because they precede and uphold the other virtues.

What are the capital virtues?
Seven virtues opposed to the seven capital sins.

Which are they ?
Humility, liberality, chastity, charity, temperance, meekness and zeal.

What are the virtues of perfection ?
The practice of the evangelical counsels, like voluntary poverty, perpetual chastity, abstinence of all intoxicating drink, &c.

www.ingramcontent.com/pod-product-compliance
Lightning Source LLC
Chambersburg PA
CBHW031930060726
47496CB00008BA/2783